CROW NOT CROW

written by Jane Yolen and Adam Stemple

illustrated by Elizabeth Dulemba

The**Cornell**Lab Publishing Group

Designed by Patricia Mitter
Edited by Kevin J. McGowan

Library of Congress Cataloging-in-Publication Data available.

ISBN: 978-1-943645-31-2

Printed in Canada

10 9 8 7 6 5 4 3 2 1

Produced by the Cornell Lab Publishing Group
120A North Salem Street
Apex, NC 27502

www.CornellLabPG.com

CPSIA tracking label information
Production Location: Friesens Corporation,
Altona, Manitoba, Canada
Production Date: 6/15/2018
Cohort: Batch No. 244542

MIX
Paper from
responsible sources
FSC® C016245
FSC
www.fsc.org

By buying products with the FSC label you are supporting the growth of responsible
forest management worldwide.

For Betsy, the first to use the
Crow Not Crow method.
—JY and AS

For my grandmother, Gammeo,
who taught me to love birds.
And for Stan, always.
—ED

The first day Dad took me out birding,
the sky was the color of Mom's old pearl ring.
The trees were draped with birds.
It was very noisy.

My brothers all love to go out birding with Dad.
They don't have any trouble telling one bird from another.
But to me, birds look pretty much the same—wings, beak, and legs.
And sometimes when I see them flying far away, they are just blurs against the sky.
"Maybe the boys have better eyes," I said.

Dad handed me a pair of small binoculars
just the right size for my hands.
"Your eyes are fine," he told me.
"You just have to learn how to see, and what to look for."

He pointed to a line of bugs at my feet.
"What do you see there?"
"Ants."

"And there?" he said, pointing up at a tree where a squirrel
with its tail raised like an umbrella, sat on a sturdy limb.
"A squirrel."

"And there?"
He pointed out at the meadow where birds hopped on the ground
and perched in the trees and soared across the morning sky.
"Birds?" I asked.
Dad nodded. "It all begins with Crow Not Crow."
"What begins?"
"Birding," he said.

We trudged into the meadow. All around us birds were singing. Hollering, really.
As we walked through the grass, we scared some of the birds up into the air.
Before I was able to get my binoculars up to my eyes, those birds were gone.
"Fast," I whispered.

But one bird didn't fly off.
It was as black as a night without any moon or stars. Sitting on
a tree branch, the bird glared down at me and opened its beak.
"Caw! Caw!" it said.
Dad pointed at it. "Crow," he said.
"Crow," I repeated. And smiled, just a little.

"Now find him in your binoculars,"
Dad whispered, as we knelt carefully
to make ourselves small.
"And be very still."

The only parts of me moving now were my
arms as I put the binoculars up to my eyes.
The crow was suddenly huge.
"Tell me what you see," Dad said.
"A big black bird."
"Is it all black?"

The crow was so big, I had to
move the binoculars around to see all of him.
"His wings are black."
I took a deep breath. "His legs are black."
I took another look. "Even his beak is black!"
"And . . ." Dad whispered.
"He's all black!" I whispered back.
"All."

Lowering my binoculars, I watched him fly away.
His wing tips spread out like long black fingers.
"Crow." I named it.
Owned it.

We walked through the meadow to a marshy stream. A black bird with a red and yellow band on its wing like a medal of war sat on a cattail.
"He's very black," I said. "Crow?"

"Did the crow have a red medallion on his wing?
Think back to what you saw before. Picture it in your head."
I thought about the crow.
All black. Black legs, black beak, black wings. Black. I shook my head.
"Not crow," Dad said.

A flock of black birds settled into a field beyond the stream.
I put my binoculars up.
Their feathers were dotted with white, like stars in the night sky.
"Crow?"
I didn't take my binoculars off of them.

"What color are their beaks?" Dad asked, even though
I was sure he knew the answer.
"Yellow," I said. "And they have stars on their feathers."
"Not crow," Dad said.

I looked at the Not Crows and tried to really see them.
Their yellow beaks. Their night-sky feathers.
I spotted one in the flock that was different. It had plain black feathers and a dark beak.
"Hey!" I whispered loudly. "There's a different bird in there."
Taking a deep breath, I steadied my binoculars.

"It's all black!"
"Is it?"
I looked again. Squinted. Stared.
At last I said, "No. Its head is brown."
"Not crow," Dad said.
"Not crow," I repeated.

A bird called from a nearby tree.
"Chuck! Chuck!" it said.
It was so close that I barely needed my binoculars.
"It's all black!" I whispered. "Its wings are black.
Its legs are black. Even its beak is black!"
I put down my binoculars and grinned up at Dad.
"Crow!"
He shook his head. "Look again."

I stared at the bird as it chuck-chucked at me.
It was all black. All! But it was Not Crow.
I tried to see the differences between Crow and this bird.
Really see them.
"It's . . . too small?"
"It's too small," Dad agreed.
"It's . . . the wrong shape?"
Dad nodded. "Wrong shape."
"And its eye is bright!" I shouted,
which made the bird fly off.
"Crow's eye is all black."
Dad smiled. "You remembered."
 I nodded. "I did."

"Not crow!"
I yelled, pointing at the fork-tailed birds twisting over the meadow.
"Not crow!" at a yellow bird on a fence post with a vee on its chest.
"Not crow!" at a wide-winged bird soaring over our heads.
I laughed and ran and Dad took big steps to keep up.
"Not crow!" I called to the tiny bird with the bandit mask.
"Not crow!" to the tiny bird with the black cap and beard.
"Not crow!" to the gray bird with the flashing wings.

Suddenly, there he was.
Peering with one black eye down at me
from the branch of a maple tree.
"Caw! Caw!" he said.

"Crow."
I named him.
Dad agreed. "Crow."
"Crow!" I said. "I see him, Dad. I really see him."
"I know," Dad said. He put his hand on my shoulder,
but lightly so he wouldn't shake my binoculars.
"I see him too."

Eventually, my binoculars got heavy.
Eventually, the crow flew off.
Eventually we headed for home,
sometimes walking,
sometimes pretending to fly.

On the bird feeder near our kitchen windows sat a red bird with a tiny crest on its head.
"Not crow," I said, a bit out of breath.
We'd walked a long way. And birding is hard work.
Seeing—really seeing—is even harder.

But this afternoon or maybe tomorrow, I might learn a new bird.
Maybe sparrow, not sparrow. Maybe owl, not owl. And the next day—another.

Till I'm as good a birder as my brothers.
Or better.

CROW

. . . .

AMERICAN CROW

Corvus brachyrhynchos

American Crows are big black birds with a distinctive cawing call.

They are highly intelligent and communicate with each other in a complex (for animals) language. Some species of crows even use tools! They live in extended and close family groups. In fact, younger crows often stay home with their parents for several years, helping them raise more young crows. Crows eat almost anything, allowing them to thrive whether in the wild or in close quarters with humans where they often find leftovers from picnics or bird feeders.

 Listen to the American Crow!

Learn more about the American Crow!

Not Crows

Photo by © Brian E. Kushner

Red-winged Blackbird
Agelaius phoeniceus

Easily identified by its distinctive red and yellow "epaulets," the Red-winged Blackbird is a fiercely territorial blackbird common throughout North America. The males often sit high on a cattail in a marsh and sing to warn other birds to stay out of their territory—a territory that can be as large as 21,000 square feet—that's a lot of territory to patrol! (Though it varies a great deal.)

Listen!

Photo by Mark Eden/GBBC

European Starling
Sturnus vulgaris

The European Starling has white spots on its body feathers. Starlings didn't exist in North America until they were introduced in the nineteenth century. Since then, the starling's aggressiveness has allowed it to become one of the most abundant birds around. Large flocks of starlings have been known to travel in a "murmuration," where they seem to move together as one gigantic creature in the sky.

Listen!

Photo by Errol Taskin/FeederWatch

Brown-headed Cowbird
Molothrus ater

The Brown-headed Cowbird is a small blackbird with a brown head that feeds on the ground with other birds, usually starlings and blackbirds. Female cowbirds don't build their own nests and lay their eggs in nests of other birds who end up raising a cowbird chick. Sometimes the other mother is half the size of her adopted chick!

Listen!

Photo by Charlie Lentz/GBBC

Common Grackle
Quiscalus quiscula

Common Grackles are large, iridescent blackbirds with a long tail. They are often seen in big flocks flying or foraging on lawns and making a lot of noise. Grackling, perhaps. Very social birds, they flock with other blackbirds, cowbirds, and starlings, especially in winter. You can identify them by their long tails, sometimes folded down the middle into a shallow V shape when they fly.

Listen!

Also pictured in this book as Not Crows

Photo by © Brian E. Kushner

Barn Swallow
Hirundo rustica

The Barn Swallow is the only North American swallow with a long forked tail, making it easy to identify whether resting or in flight. However, swallows rarely rest, spending most of their time swooping and diving for insects to eat, sometimes high in the sky, sometimes barely a foot above the ground. They make their nests out of mud that sticks to buildings, including, of course, barns.

Listen!

Photo by Mark Eden/GBBC

Eastern Meadowlark
Sturnella magna

Its bright yellow breast with a black chevron, or V, makes the Eastern Meadowlark easily distinguishable from all other birds except the Western Meadowlark, to which it is nearly identical. While on the ground feeding, its brown speckled back serves as excellent camouflage. Lucky for birders, it likes to sit on fence posts and sing loudly, its bright yellow chest puffed out proudly.

Listen!

Photo by © Brian E. Kushner

Red-tailed Hawk
Buteo jamaicensis

Often seen soaring over fields or perched up high near a roadway, the Red-tailed Hawk is the most abundant hawk in North America. Red-tailed hawks are members of the genus *Buteo*, hawks known for broad, rounded wings and a short, wide tail. Their tails are usually more a chestnut color than bright red, and some are not red at all.

Listen!

Photo by Lou Orr/GBBC

Common Yellowthroat
Geothlypis trichas

You'll probably hear its distinctive song before you ever spy this masked bandit. Common Yellowthroats tend to skulk about in dense undergrowth searching for small insects and spiders, or calling out *witchety, witchety, witchety.* Suspicious behavior indeed!

Listen!

Photo by Jerry Acton/GBBC

BLACK-CAPPED CHICKADEE
Poecile atricapillus

If this tiny bird didn't get its name from its call of *chick-a-dee-deedee*, it would probably be called "The Curious Bird." It is curious about everything. And if it finds something interesting, it will often get other birds to join in the investigation. It is universally considered "cute" thanks to its oversized round head and tiny body.

Listen!

Photo by Maria Corcacas/GBBC

NORTHERN MOCKINGBIRD
Mimus polyglottos

So named for its ability to "mock" other birds' songs, the Northern Mockingbird sings through strings of other birds' songs constantly, sometimes all through the night. It is a bland gray bird when perched, but in flight it reveals bright white patches on its wings that flash when they flap.

Listen!

Photo by Charles Rose, IV/FeederWatch

NORTHERN CARDINAL
Cardinalis cardinalis

The bright red plumage that gives the cardinal its name (from the scarlet robes of cardinals in the Catholic church) makes the Northern Cardinal easy to spot and identify—especially since it doesn't fly south or change plumage in the winter like many birds do.

Listen!

LISTEN, WATCH, AND LEARN WITH OUR FREE BIRD QR APP!

Download on the **App Store**　　ANDROID APP ON **Google** play

BIRD QR is a free book companion app created especially for *Crow Not Crow* and other books from the Cornell Lab Publishing Group.

Knowing which birds are out there is important to scientists. Sometimes scientists don't use just their eyes, but listen to identify birds. Using the QR codes in this book, you could also learn to identify birds by how they sound. Learn which birds are around you, even if you can't see them!

HAVE YOU EVER WONDERED, "WHAT IS THAT BIRD?"

Let the free Merlin® Bird ID app help you solve the mystery! It makes bird ID easier by showing you the birds in your own area that match what you've seen. Download this free app at *Merlin.AllAboutBirds.org*.

The Cornell Lab of Ornithology

The Cornell Lab of Ornithology is a world leader in the study, appreciation, and conservation of birds. As with all Cornell Lab Publishing Group books, 35 percent of the net proceeds from the sale of *Crow Not Crow* will directly support the Cornell Lab's projects such as children's educational and community programs.